anythink

D1095477

DOWN BY THE STATION

Retold by STEVEN ANDERSON

Illustrated by GAIA BORDICCHIA

CANTATA
LEARNING

MANKATO, MINNESOTA

WWW.CANTATALEARNING.COM

**CANTATA
LEARNING**

MANKATO, MINNESOTA

Published by Cantata Learning
1710 Roe Crest Drive
North Mankato, MN 56003
www.cantatalearning.com

Library of Congress Control Number: 2014957018
978-1-63290-285-6 (hardcover/CD)
978-1-63290-437-9 (paperback/CD)
978-1-63290-479-9 (paperback)

Down by the Station by Steven Anderson
Illustrated by Gaia Bordicchia

Book design, Tim Palin Creative
Editorial direction, Flat Sole Studio
Executive musical production and direction, Elizabeth Draper
Music arranged and produced by Steven C Music

Printed in the United States of America.

VISIT
WWW.CANTATALEARNING.COM/ACCESS-OUR-MUSIC
TO SING ALONG TO THE SONG

All aboard! The train is about ready to leave

the **station**! Are you ready to take a train ride?

Now turn the page, and sing along.

Down by the station,

Early in the morning,

See the little **pufferbellies**

All in a row.

See the station master
Turn the little handle.

Chug, chug, puff, puff!
Off they go!

Down by the station,

Early in the morning,

See the shiny train cars

All in a row.

Waiting to get hitched up
And go on their adventure.

Chug, chug, puff, puff!
Off they go!

Down by the station,

Early in the morning,

Climb on board,

And hear the whistle blow.

Mr. **Conductor**,

Please take my **ticket**.

Chug, chug, puff, puff!

Off they go!

Down by the station,

Early in the morning,

See the little pufferbellies

All in a row.

See the station master
Turn the little handle.

Chug, chug, puff, puff!
Off they go!

SONG LYRICS
Down by the Station

Down by the station,
Early in the morning,
See the little pufferbellies
All in a row.

See the station master
Turn the little handle.

Chug, chug, puff, puff!
Off they go!

Down by the station,
Early in the morning,
See the shiny train cars
All in a row.

Waiting to get hitched up
And go on their adventure.

Chug, chug, puff, puff!
Off they go!

Down by the station,
Early in the morning,
Climb on board,
And hear the whistle blow.

Mr. Conductor,
Please take my ticket.

Chug, chug, puff, puff!
Off they go!

Down by the station,
Early in the morning,
See the little pufferbellies
All in a row.

See the station master
Turn the little handle.

Chug, chug, puff, puff!
Off they go!

Down by the Station

Americana
Steven C Music

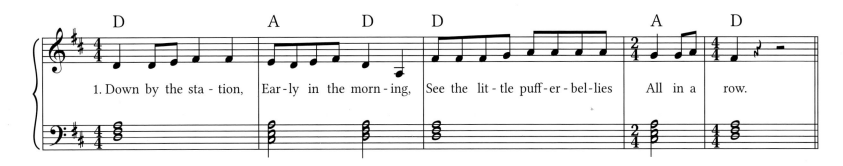

1. Down by the sta - tion, Early in the morn - ing, See the lit - tle puff-er - bel-lies All in a row.

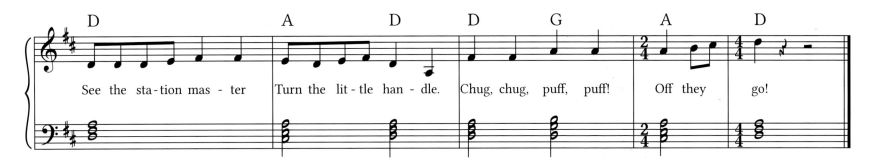

See the sta - tion mas - ter Turn the lit - tle han - dle. Chug, chug, puff, puff! Off they go!

Verse 2
Down by the station,
Early in the morning,
See the shiny train cars
All in a row.

Waiting to get hitched up
And go on their adventure.

Chug, chug, puff, puff!
Off they go!

Verse 3
Down by the station,
Early in the morning,
Climb on board,
And hear the whistle blow.

Mr. Conductor,
Please take my ticket.

Chug, chug, puff, puff!
Off they go!

Verse 4
Down by the station,
Early in the morning,
See the little pufferbellies
All in a row.

See the station master
Turn the little handle.

Chug, chug, puff, puff!
Off they go!

GLOSSARY

conductor—a person who drives a train

pufferbelly—the name for a train engine powered by steam

station—a place or building where a certain service is based; a train station is where trains stop to pick up people and let them off.

ticket—a piece of paper that shows you have paid for an event or service; people need to buy tickets to ride a train.

GUIDED READING ACTIVITIES

1. Where do you think the trains in this book are going?

2. What does the conductor do in this book?

3. Pretend you are going on an adventure on a train. Draw a picture of the train you are riding on. Where are you going, and what are you bringing with you?

TO LEARN MORE

Klein, Adria F. *Big Train Takes a Trip*. Minneapolis, MN: Stone Arch Books, 2014.

Richardson, Adele D. *Freight Trains in Action*. North Mankato, MN: Capstone Press, 2012.

Rogers, Hal. *Trains*. Mankato, MN: Child's World, 2014.

Sheilds, Amy. *Trains*. Washington, DC: National Geographic Children's Books, 2012.